The MOST PRECIOUS GIFT

A Story of the Nativity

MARTY CRISP · **FLOYD COOPER**

PHILOMEL BOOKS

To Liam
From Granna—M.C.

This is for my Texas fam:
Cathy, Mick, and Roland—F.C.

PHILOMEL BOOKS
A division of Penguin Young Readers Group
Published by The Penguin Group
Penguin Group (USA) Inc., 375 Hudson Street, New York, NY 10014, U.S.A.
Penguin Group (Canada), 90 Eglinton Avenue East, Suite 700, Toronto,
Ontario, Canada M4P 2Y3 (a division of Pearson Penguin Canada Inc.)
Penguin Books Ltd, 80 Strand, London WC2R 0RL, England.
Penguin Ireland, 25 St. Stephen's Green, Dublin 2, Ireland
(a division of Penguin Books Ltd.)
Penguin Group (Australia), 250 Camberwell Road, Camberwell,
Victoria 3124, Australia (a division of Pearson Australia Group Pty Ltd).
Penguin Books India Pvt Ltd, 11 Community Centre, Panchsheel Park,
New Delhi - 110 017, India.
Penguin Group (NZ), Cnr Airborne and Rosedale Roads, Albany,
Auckland 1310, New Zealand (a division of Pearson New Zealand Ltd).
Penguin Books (South Africa) (Pty) Ltd, 24 Sturdee Avenue, Rosebank,
Johannesburg 2196, South Africa.
Penguin Books Ltd, Registered Offices: 80 Strand, London WC2R 0RL, England.

Manufactured in China by South China Printing Co. Ltd.
Design by Katrina Damkoehler. Text set in Calisto MT Bold.

Library of Congress Cataloging-in-Publication Data
Crisp, Marty. The most precious gift : a story of the Nativity / by Marty Crisp ;
illustrated by Floyd Cooper. p. cm. Summary: While traveling to Bethlehem
with his beloved dog, a young servant to one of the Magi worries about finding
a gift to give the baby Jesus.
1. Jesus Christ—Nativity—Juvenile fiction. [1. Jesus Christ—Nativity—Fiction.
2. Dogs—Fiction. 3. Household employees—Fiction.] I. Cooper, Floyd, ill. II. Title.
PZ7.C86942Mos 2006   [E]—dc22   2005034806   ISBN 0-399-24296-1

10 9 8 7 6 5 4 3 2 1
First Impression

As much as he thought about it,
Ameer had no idea what to give
the Wondrous Being they
had set out to find.
And time was running out.

Ameer's king had been advised to "follow the star" to find the Magical Baby so long foretold. But stars were forever blinking on and off in the night sky. Ameer felt much safer following his dog, Ṛa.

Ra might only be the dog of a third assistant kennel keeper, but he had the best nose in all the Eastern Kingdoms. He often ranged in front of the caravan, as if he knew exactly where they were going.

Ameer, however, trudged along in back, his feet dragging as he tried to think of something—*anything*—that might make a worthy gift.

When Ra trotted back to walk beside him, Ameer talked to the dog about it.

"Everyone has a present for the New King. The tent steward has a fine carpet, the robe maker a bolt of his best cloth. The woodcutter fashioned a staff of braided river willow, and the bird keeper taught a parrot to say 'Hail to the King.' But what can *I* give, Ra? What?"

Ameer had nothing to offer except a ragged scarf he'd caught, sailing on a desert wind. It was ragged because Ra liked to play tug-of-war with it.

It had been a week since the breadfruit and bananas were
heaped in baskets, the peacocks and pheasants shoved into cages,
and the wineskins filled to bursting. Pairs of bullocks strained to
pull the heavy sledges, so loaded down that their runners cut deep
lines in the desert sand.

The old king rode in a silver chaise atop the largest camel.
Lesser noblemen rode smaller camels. Everyone else walked.
Soon, two more kings joined the journey, and the caravan became
a flowing city, pouring across the desert.

When they all stopped for a meal, Ameer shared his own small ration of boiled egg and date bread with Ra. The two friends shared everything.

Ra had been the runt of a royal litter of coursing hounds, and all runts were thrown into the river by order of the kennel master. But Ameer had looked into the amber eyes of the pup and known he must save it.

So, when the kennel keeper tossed a sack into the reeds at the shallow edge of the river, Ameer was waiting. As soon as the keeper turned away, Ameer hooked the sack with a long pole.

Ameer named his rescued puppy Ra. He thought the dog's
white coat blazed like the rays of Ra, the sun god. He volunteered
to watch the royal goat herd at night, in exchange for milk. When
he wasn't mucking out kennels, Ameer stole moments to train
Ra, rewarding him with hugs and words of praise.

Ra grew into such a fine dog that the kennel keeper tried
to reclaim him. But Ra refused to obey any voice but Ameer's.
Angry, the kennel keeper pulled out a whip to strike the
disobedient dog, but Ameer hurled himself between.
He still bore a scar from that whip stroke on his cheek.

"Fah!" the kennel keeper had sneered. "You are
a stupid boy and this is a worthless dog." As the
kennel keeper stamped away, Ra licked Ameer's
wound until they both felt better. If only
Ameer felt better now.

Instead, he felt ashamed.

"It is impossible," Ameer confided to Ra. "Our king is giving the Wondrous One a golden chalice. Another king carries a jeweled case filled with a yellow block of frankincense, big enough to light a whole palace. The third has a silver bowl filled with the red resin of the camphor tree. Everyone says camphor myrrh can cure any ailment from toothache to fever. There simply cannot be finer gifts than these, Ra. Perhaps if I were a great seer, I would know what to do. But I am only third assistant kennel keeper, and can see no further than the end of the rake I use to gather soiled straw." Ameer fell asleep, still pondering the problem, his head pillowed on Ra's side.

A full fourteen days had passed
by the time the great caravan stopped in a field
next to the small village of Bethlehem.

Ameer had made up his mind. He would not
allow himself to see the Baby King. He would
wait outside instead.

Ameer looked around. The town was not
what he'd expected. There were only ordinary
houses and shops. No palaces at all.

The three kings walked over to the crude
stable behind the town's only inn, ducking
under the sloped thatched roof to enter.

"Get in line! Line up!" shouted a burly
overseer, trying to bring order to the chaos
that swirled around the great caravan. He
shoved Ameer, with Ra at his heels, into line.
Ameer knew he should move to the side, but
the crowd pushed forward, carrying them along,
until finally, Ameer had no choice but to bend and
go through the low stable door.

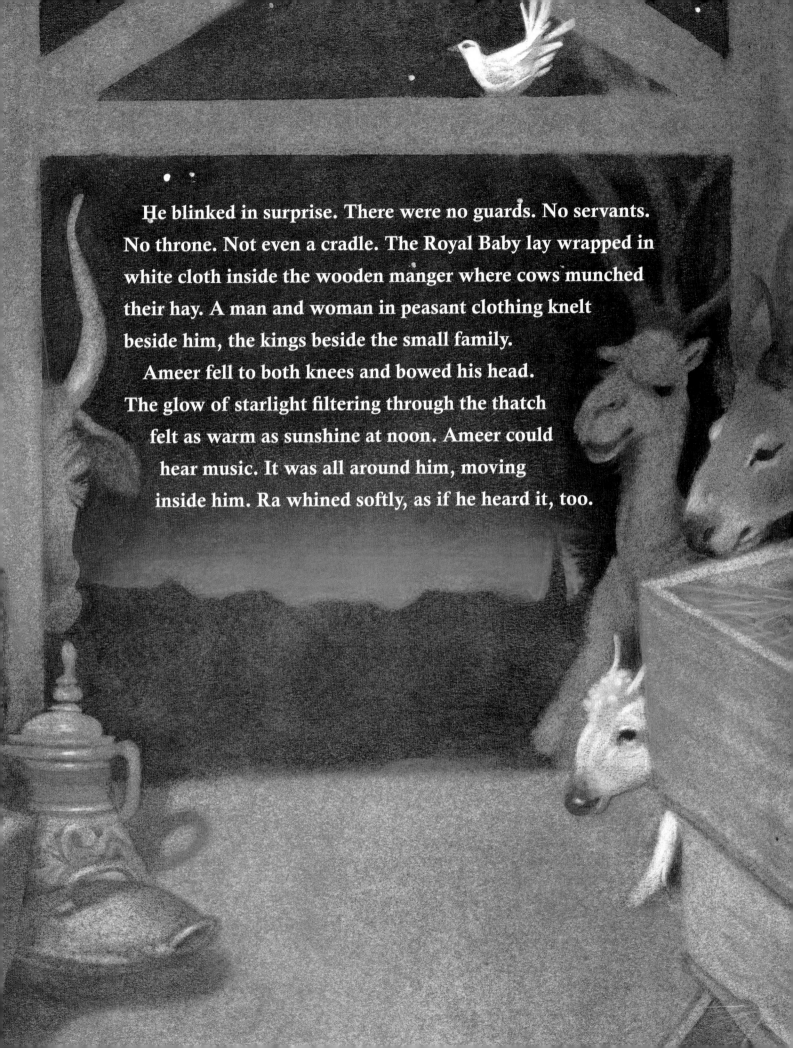

He blinked in surprise. There were no guards. No servants. No throne. Not even a cradle. The Royal Baby lay wrapped in white cloth inside the wooden manger where cows munched their hay. A man and woman in peasant clothing knelt beside him, the kings beside the small family.

Ameer fell to both knees and bowed his head. The glow of starlight filtering through the thatch felt as warm as sunshine at noon. Ameer could hear music. It was all around him, moving inside him. Ra whined softly, as if he heard it, too.

"Move along! Make room!" shouted a voice from somewhere outside.

"But—*I* have a gift," Ameer blurted. He laid a trembling hand on Ra, leaning close to whisper in the dog's ear. Then Ameer looked shyly at the Baby's mother. "Here is my dog, Ra. He is a very good dog. He is my best friend. I promise he will watch over you and keep you safe." Ameer stood up before he could change his mind.

Ameer's king shook his head in disapproval, coming forward and laying a hand on Ameer's arm. "It is not wise to give *all* you own, boy," he said in his deep voice. "For what, then, will you have left?"

But the Baby's mother reached out a gentle hand and touched them both—kennel boy and king. "Of all these gifts," she said softly, looking at Ameer and gesturing toward the mound of presents with the kings' gold, frankincense and myrrh sitting on top, "yours is most precious."

The Baby's mother moved her hand to stroke Ra's head. The Baby reached out a chubby fist and tried to put Ra's ear in his mouth.

The Baby's mother smiled at Ameer. "You have given all you have. That is what my Son has come to ask of every man. Though few will do it."

Ameer's face had grown hot. There was something salty on his lips: his own tears. He hadn't even known he was crying. "Take care of Ra," Ameer said, fighting to keep his voice steady. "He is"—Ameer paused—"the Son Dog."

Ameer and Ra looked at each other one last time. Then Ameer turned on his heel and fled blindly from the stable. Ra barked once—a good-bye.

So it came to pass that God blessed Ameer, just as Mary,
the Holy Child's mother, had promised. As he grew to
manhood, Ameer became the most respected seer in all the
Eastern Kingdoms, with a vision as pure and true as his heart.

As for Ra, he led the Baby's family from Israel to safety in Egypt, watching over the Christ Child always. And every night, Ameer looked up to the dark sky. For, as the Christmas Star faded, the Dog Star took its place.

It glows there still, the brightest star in all God's heaven.

Author's Note

*The fact that a white dog is seen again and again in 14th–16th century paintings of the Nativity (**The Face in the Corner**, Robin Gibson, National Portrait Gallery, 1998) fascinated me. In searching many sources, I discovered dozens of such paintings by Old Masters, from Stefano da Verona (1375) and Bartolo di Fredi (1380) to Botticelli (1474) and Jan Gossaert (1503). The dog continued to appear in later paintings, such as **Christ Healing the Blind Man** (El Greco, 1560) and **The Supper at Emmaus** (Titian, 1535). A symbol? Perhaps. A real dog? For a God who willingly became a man, what better companion could there be?*

—Marty Crisp